Animals That JUMP

by Pearl Markovics

Consultant:
Beth Gambro
Reading Specialist
Yorkville, Illinois

Contents

Animals That Jump.........2

Key Words...............16

Index....................16

About the Author..........16

New York, New York

Animals That Jump

What can jump?

A frog can jump.

What can jump?

A goat can jump.

What can jump?

A fox can jump.

What can jump?

A rabbit can jump.

What can jump?

A grasshopper can jump.

What can jump?

12

A kangaroo can jump.

Can you jump?

Yes, you can!

Key Words

fox

frog

goat

grasshopper

kangaroo

rabbit

Index

fox 6–7
frog 2–3
goat 4–5
grasshopper 10–11
kangaroo 12–13
rabbit 8–9

About the Author

Pearl Markovics loves to see how far—and how high—she can jump.